The Happy Acres Haunted Hotel for Active Seniors

We finally reached Ward 12. "M and N are across the hall from each other?" Samuel asked. "Is that because the first half of the alphabet is on one side of the hall and the second half is on the other?"

"If I find out that you memorized a schematic of the building before you arrived I'm going to be very disappointed. Yes."

"So you have the room at the very end of the hall and therefore the building?"

"Yes indeed."

"Hmmm."

"What?"

"You seem like someone who would prefer to be in the middle of everything, not at the highest, farthest, most isolated part of the entire facility."

"Ah. Well, as to that…just wait until dark."

D1522339

The Happy Acres Haunted Hotel For Active Seniors

By Gini Koch

The Happy Acres Haunted Hotel for Active Seniors
Published by Gini Koch at CreateSpace

Editors: Mary Fiore and Veronica Cook
Cover Artist: Lisa Dovichi

Second Edition
ISBN: 978-1-48405-5328

Gini Koch
http://www.ginikoch.com

Dedication

To the memory of my Gramma Julie who truly was Mattie in real life.

Acknowledgments

Thanks as always to my wonderful agent, Cherry Weiner, and my super crit partner, Lisa Dovichi. Much love as always to my husband, Steve, and daughter, Veronica. But most of all, love to the memory of my grandmother, Julia, who faced everything, even ghosts, with a cheerful demeanor that concealed a loving, iron will. I miss you, Gramma, every day, and I could not have written this story without you in my life.

Janice raced over as fast as her walker would allow. It had rollers on it, so, all things considered, it was pretty fast. "New meat!" she said in a stage whisper. "Being checked in right now. He looks somewhere in his sixties, so a young one!"

"Young being a relative term."

Janice giggled. "True enough. He's not young enough for you, Mattie, but still, he's a hottie."

The rest of us looked at each other. "I'm willing to pass judgment," Trudy said. "Purely in the interests of science, of course." The rest of the girls and Joseph who, being of the gay persuasion, chose to hang with, as he put it, his side of the house, all nodded in support of the idea that we go check out the new guy.

"Works for me. Let's go see how he stacks up to Hunkman."

Betsy, who wasn't really in our group but somehow felt that if we were doing something she was automatically invited by dint of her being a nosy pain in the butt, sniffed. "His name, Mattie, is Helkman."

"Whatever, Bets." Hunkman's given name was actually Jason Helkman, but since he was as fine a specimen of manhood as I'd ever seen – and I'd seen a lot – I'd christened him Hunkman when he'd come to work at our Happy Acres Senior Living Hotel. Shocking only Betsy, he didn't mind the nickname.

Joseph rolled his eyes then sighed. "What are the odds the new one's playing for my side of the team?"

"Couldn't tell," Janice said. "He's well dressed and groomed, so your odds are better than average."

"A man can dream," Joseph said hopefully.

We made our way from the Sun Terrace into the Main Lobby. This made it sound a lot more attractive than the Home actually was. It was a big, blocky T-shaped building with five stories going up and two going down. Conveniently, we had our own morgue in the basement level. Not because we were all that close to death, but because this place was a converted hospital.

New arrivals were always greeted with interest and as we passed other residents, they joined us. By the time we reached the Main Lobby we had quite the mob formed. If our new arrival had a weak heart he wasn't going to last long here anyway, so might as well scare the crap out of him now and get it over with.

Sure enough, there was a new man standing there, getting the Cheerful Overview that Mrs. Wilson insisted on making every new resident hear, whether they wanted to or not.

Mrs. Wilson was one of those well-meaning women who think that just because they care about a cause and work for that cause it allows them to treat the individuals who make up that cause as part of a major dog and pony show. She was also of the opinion that if those Individuals of the Cause weren't necessary to whatever show was going on, we were all better in the Not Heard and Preferably Not Seen category.

Right now, we were clearly supposed to be silent, because she shot me a look I was quite familiar with – her "shut up or I pay someone to smother you in your sleep" look.

"Has she told you what this place was before it was 'revitalized'?" I asked the fresh meat. As males went, Janice hadn't been exaggerating. He was tall, broad, and definitely had a twinkle or two still left in his bright, blue eyes. Full head of neatly combed silver hair. Nice clothes that fit him perfectly. Either he'd been a C.E.O. – which I doubted, because most C.E.O.s didn't end up here – or my money said he was going to make Joseph a very happy man.

He smiled. Good teeth. Couldn't tell if they were real or not. Mine were, but that's because I was a flossing fanatic beloved by dentists everywhere. "Missus Wilson said it was a hotel." He winked at me, which either meant he was going to disappoint Joseph terribly or that he was fully aware of what this building had been in its so-called glory days.

Mrs. Wilson scanned the crowd. With this many witnesses, she was going to have to go for the Full Confession Introduction. She didn't care for the Full Confession Introduction, but it was my personal favorite. "I'm sorry, Mister Davidson, but you must have misheard me. It's a hotel now for our active seniors who desire companionship and mental stimulation. It, ah, used to be a hospital."

"A haunted hospital. And it only used to be a hospital. It's still haunted, trust me."

The rest of the gang nodded or murmured. You didn't live here more than a week before you knew all the ghost stories were true.

She shot the Death Glare at me again. Never worried me. I was Hunkman's favorite, for a variety of reasons. "Supposedly. However, I can assure you, Mister Davidson, that you'll find no haunts here."

"Not in the daylight, no. Our haunts are nocturnal."

"I've never seen them," Mrs. Wilson snapped. "Ever."

"For some reason the haunts don't care for Missus Wilson. Shocking us all."

"Really, Missus Mattingly, you're being very rude." Mrs. Wilson loved to tell me I was rude, as if I wasn't aware of when I was pointedly being rude or not. She reminded me of my first mother-in-law. I'd hated my first mother-in-law.

"You're so right!" I trotted over and put my hand out. "I'm pleased to meet Hugh Jackman himself."

He grinned widely as he took my hand and squeezed it gently. "You have a silver tongue, don't you? Samuel Davidson, at your service, Missus Mattingly."

"Oh, call me Mattie. Everyone other than certain people who shall remain nameless because they're standing right here calls me Mattie."

"With pleasure. And please call me Samuel."

"Happy to." I didn't share that I'd planned to anyway, permission given or not. I let go of his hand. "You alone or part of a set?"

"A set? Oh! No, my wife passed away several years ago now." He looked a little misty for a moment but recovered. I could feel Joseph's disappointment and without looking behind me I knew all the girls had moved a step closer and all the other men were muttering to themselves about the unfairness of life. I hadn't been offering idle flattery – Samuel looked a *lot* like Hugh Jackman. I approved.

"I've buried three husbands myself."

"Three?" Samuel looked a little nervous.

"Oh, no need to look so worried. Didn't kill them for the insurance money, and you can take that as fact because if I had, I'd be living in a mansion in Santa Barbara right now, not hanging out at the Haunted Former Hospital."

"Ah…" Samuel said, seeming suddenly out of his depth. Pity. I liked the lookers, but I preferred a sharp mind. Hunkman was far too smart to be working here, but he had his reasons, and his brain made his face and body even better looking. Sure he was young enough to be my son, okay, grandson, but I was older, not dead. And seeing as I saw dead people all the time, I was in a great position to verify that I still had a pulse and couldn't walk through walls.

"Missus Mattingly is joking about where she'd choose to live," Mrs. Wilson added quickly. "Happy Acres is the finest elder care hotel in all of Southern California."

"Well, in all of Boyle Heights, and that's something, right?"

Samuel stared at me for a long moment, then he burst out laughing. "Well put. I think I'll fit right in around here."

Mrs. Wilson looked relieved. "So glad to hear it."

A young woman came in, dragging a couple of huge rolling suitcases behind her. She was tall and slender, quite pretty, with long blonde hair and big blue eyes. I knew who she belonged to before she spoke. "Granddad, are you sure you don't want more of your stuff?"

She stopped and seemed to notice the rest of us for the first time. "Oh! I'm so sorry. I didn't mean to interrupt your meeting." She looked embarrassed and her abrupt stop caused her to lose control of one of the suitcases, which promptly flopped over. The Main Lobby had faux marble floors and fairly good acoustics. The luggage made quite the audible impression.

She grabbed for it, and lost control of the other suitcase, which followed suit and fell over, naturally, in the opposite direction. Her face was bright red by now.

Samuel went over to help her, as did Joseph and a couple of the other men. "I'm *so* sorry," she said, sounding ready to commit a minor form of suicide.

"These things happen," Mrs. Wilson said, making it clear that they weren't appreciated things and they didn't happen all that often.

I snorted as loudly as I could, which was pretty loud. I practiced. "Oh, honey, don't worry. This is about the most excitement any of us have had for weeks. And we weren't having a meeting. We're all here to check your grandfather out, and I mean that in all the ways you can take it."

She stared at me for a moment, then she started to giggle. So it was a family thing. Good. Hopefully it merely indicated that the Davidson clan liked to ensure they were really laughing at a joke, not that it took them a while to catch the drift.

Samuel and Joseph righted one of the suitcases, and Samuel turned and smiled at me. "This is my only grandchild, Sarah. Who," he gave her a stern look, "was supposed to leave these in the car for me to get once all the paperwork was done."

"I don't want you straining," she said quietly.

"Bad heart?" Joseph asked, with a touch of concern. Yeah, I didn't want to lose our own Hugh Jackman lookalike quickly either.

"Oh, no," Samuel said. "Sarah just worries too much about me."

"You don't need to move in here, Granddad," Sarah said. "I've heard rumors…"

"They're all true," I shared. This earned me a worried look from Sarah and a displeased one from Mrs. Wilson. "However, we know how to deal with our extra guests."

"And you need to plan your wedding without having me underfoot," Samuel added.

Sarah didn't look convinced. However, this was an area where Mrs. Wilson excelled – ensuring that whoever checked in never checked out. So to speak.

"Your grandfather deserves the opportunity to spend time with lovely, active people of his own generation," Mrs. Wilson said with just the right combination of grandeur, sternness, warmth, and teasing in her tone. I knew she had to practice that, because once you lived here, you never heard this tone again. Or maybe it was just me.

"I suppose." Sarah didn't sound convinced.

"It's not as if I'll be that far away," Samuel said. "I have my car so I'll have full mobility."

"You have a car?" Betsy said. "That's so wonderful."

"Yes, cars are something we've never had here at the Home." I ensured I got a lot of sarcasm into that sentence.

Samuel and Sarah both laughed. Betsy sniffed at me. Mrs. Wilson, however, shot me another icy look. "Perhaps you'd like to show Mister Davidson around, Missus Mattingly?"

This was a new one. Mrs. Wilson normally preferred to do the big walkthrough herself. Perhaps she wanted Samuel out of the way so she could ensure Sarah wasn't going to grab her grandfather and run.

"I live for this kind of opportunity. What room is Mister Davidson going to be spending the rest of his golden years inside?"

"Twelve A."

Well, the mystery was explained. I lived in 12 B, so Samuel was my new neighbor.

"Come with me, mister, and don't talk to the other boys and girls."

"I think he should talk to us," Trudy said.

"We'll go with you," Janice said. "So you don't get lost."

"I'm in," Joseph added. "Always nice to make the new tenants feel welcome."

The rest of the gang appeared ready to help me escort Samuel upstairs. I had no objection, though we weren't all going to fit into the elevator in one group.

Mrs. Wilson cleared her throat. "I think, under the circumstances, it might be nice for all of you to stay and reassure our newest friend's granddaughter that her grandfather has made the perfect choice for his new living arrangements."

There was some under-the-breath muttering, but everyone recognized Mrs. Wilson's tone. It was her "do this or I ensure that the tapioca has something 'extra' in it that you won't enjoy" voice.

"Let's leave Nurse Ratched to her fun. Someone will bring Sarah up."

"Is she really that bad, Missus Wilson?" Samuel asked as we walked to the elevator. He wasn't moving slowly, which was nice. I was one of the faster walkers here, and it was refreshing not to have to slow to a crawl.

"No, not really. I just enjoy tormenting her."

"Keeps you young?"

"Why, Samuel, there's a little bit of snark underneath that twinkly exterior, isn't there?"

He chuckled. "I imagine I'm going to have to work hard at it, to keep up with you."

"Oh, flattery will get you everywhere. As my second husband learned."

"Mattingly was your third husband?" Samuel asked as the elevator began its journey.

"Yes. My first husband was Garvey, second was Mays, and the third was Mattingly." I waited. Much depended upon his next statements; mostly if we were going to hang or if I was going to toss him to Betsy.

Samuel cocked his head. "All your husbands were baseball players?"

He was a keeper! "Not the real ones, but good call. And we know it wasn't the real ones because, again, I'm not in that mansion in Santa Barbara."

"Were they all baseball fans?"

"Oh yes. Sports nuts, so to speak. It's a requirement I have."

"Really? Most women don't seem to care for the idea of men loving their sports."

"Well, my other requirement is that my husbands had to love said sports along with me. I was perfectly happy going to games, and a man who's watching the game with his wife in their living room isn't a man who's out at the bars or catting around."

"Interesting theory."

"Well," I said as we reached the top floor and left the elevator, "it's worked for me." The elevators let us out at the main hallway intersection, so we could go right, left, or straight. We went straight.

Samuel looked around. "You know, I'm confused. With a room numbered Twelve A, I assumed I'd be on a first floor."

"Oh, that kind of numbering is for normal people and normal retirement homes. Around here we like to mix it up and keep the senile guessing."

"I'm not senile…yet…but I'm not following you."

I shrugged as we walked down the hallway. "We're not joking about this place being haunted. The ghosts have their own numbering system. Most of them think they're still in a hospital, at least, that's what we've determined."

"You don't sound afraid."

"I'm not. The dead can't hurt you. It's the living you need to watch out for."

"Wise advice. I still don't understand why we're on the fifth floor and heading so far down the hall."

"The sections are divided. We're in Section Twelve, which is at the end portion of the fifth floor. There are sixty sections."

"Ah. Each floor is divided into twelfths?"

"Yes. Why, no one's really sure." Actually, we had a collective really good guess, but this was one of the many Test Questions we put forth to the newbies to see if they were going to fit in or need to be sent to the morgue. So to speak.

"Wards," Samuel said promptly. "This used to be a hospital, so it would make sense that parts of each floor were sectioned off."

"That makes a lot of sense."

I'd tried to sound ingenuous, but clearly I hadn't succeeded, because Samuel chuckled. "Glad to see I passed that test."

"I was that transparent?"

"No, I'm just familiar with the concept of hazing."

"I see we're at the start of a beautiful friendship."

We finally reached Ward 12. "M and N are across the hall from each other?" Samuel asked. "Is that because the first half of the alphabet is on one side of the hall and the second half is on the other?"

"If I find out that you memorized a schematic of the building before you arrived I'm going to be very disappointed. Yes."

"So you have the room at the very end of the hall and therefore the building?"

"Yes indeed."

"Hmmm."

"What?"

"You seem like someone who would prefer to be in the middle of everything, not at the highest, farthest, most isolated part of the entire facility."

"Ah. Well, as to that...just wait until dark."

It didn't take too long for Sarah to cave under Mrs. Wilson's will. She joined us fairly quickly, with a couple orderlies bringing Samuel's luggage.

I chose to be tactful – I could manage it when I wanted to – and left them alone so Samuel could get settled into his room and have some alone time with his granddaughter, who still looked ready to grab him and run.

Like mine, Samuel's room was a nice sized studio apartment. There were certain aspects of the rooms that reminded you that this place had originally been a hospital, the curtain track in the ceiling which held the curtain that went around the bed for one. This was standard for every room, single or double. For those rooms where there were two beds or a king bed, there were two curtains. It gave an illusion of privacy that Mrs. Wilson felt was important. I felt it was probably really costly to redo the ceilings so she'd chosen to improvise.

It was weird, but it made sense. Sure, this was a "hotel", but there were medical facilities in the top underground level as well as a few on the bottom/morgue level. During the day, there was plenty of activity underground, what we residents called Downstairs, seeing as the doctors cared for all the residents and took walk-ins as well.

We got the most comments about all the doctors' offices being underground from new residents and walk-in patients both, at least at first. But the lower levels were rather nice. The offices were large and, despite being underground, quite airy. Downstairs was tastefully decorated because Mrs. Wilson had controlling power over the entire facility and, much as I enjoyed tormenting her, she had a good eye for interior design.

There was underground parking for daytime medical visitors, meaning most people never had to go to the ground level or even interact with the Happy Acres residents outside of various doctors' waiting rooms.

The rents were reasonable, so we got some good medical personnel Downstairs, who rotated being on call for resident emergencies. Downstairs, despite still possessing a functioning morgue, was pleasant and comforting in its way. During the day.

Even during what everyone referred to as evening one could wander Downstairs without worry. As long as there were non-residents Downstairs, it remained a nice place to be.

At night, of course, everything changed.

At night, Happy Acres came alive.

Hunkman, by dint of being the Chief Orderly, got to choose his shifts. He always worked nights, coming on duty between the dinner shifts. The dining room really couldn't handle all the residents at one time, so those who liked to eat while the sun was still up had their dinners at 5pm, and those of us who liked to pretend we were still young and viable dined at 6:30pm. You could always alter what time you ate, but most of us stayed in our chosen timeslots, in part because we were creatures of habit and in part because that's when our friends ate.

The knock on my door came promptly at 6:15. I opened the door to see a tall, broad-shouldered, dark-haired, brown-eyed vision of male perfection. He was mixed race, meaning he had gorgeous caramel-colored skin on top of everything else.

"Hunkman, punctual as always."

He smiled. That the light didn't flash off his teeth with a "ding!" noise was probably just an oversight on the light's part. Yeah, he was that visually stunning. I was old but not dead and Hunkman could still get my pulse going merely by standing there. When he flashed the smile, it was enough to make a gal believe she was twenty-two again. It was a certain magic he had.

"Good to see you, Mattie. I understand you have a new neighbor."

"Yep. Hoping he's a keeper."

"Let's find out. He's chosen the later dinner shift."

"Another mark in his pros column."

"How many are in the cons column?"

"None so far, but he's only been here a couple of hours."

Hunkman chuckled and knocked on 12 B's door. Sarah opened it. Her jaw dropped open, she looked Hunkman up and down, managed to remember to close her mouth, swallowed, then smiled. Widely. Yep, she had the standard straight woman and gay man reaction to Hunkman.

"Can I help you?" she asked rather breathlessly.

Hunkman smiled. Sarah leaned against the doorframe. "I'm Jason Helkman, the Chief Orderly, which means I'm also the Head Nurse. We do both jobs here."

This was true, but for some archaic reason Mrs. Wilson didn't like to admit we had male nurses on staff, so she insisted they use the orderly titles. This was merely one of her many quirks. It didn't matter to any of the residents, but it made it difficult for the staff to get better jobs, which was probably why Mrs. Wilson had said quirk.

"Most of us call him Hunkman," I shared.

"I can understand why." Sarah blushed the moment the words left her mouth.

Hunkman was used to it, of course, and he took the compliment in stride. "Thank you. I'm here to collect Samuel for dinner."

"Oh. Granddad is just freshening up. Would you like to come in? I'm sure he'll only be a minute more."

We entered and Sarah trotted over to gather her purse. I looked up at Hunkman. He was watching her, and his expression was one I recognized – I'd seen him look at someone else like this, but only the one – interest mixed with longing.

"You know, Sarah," I said, "you're welcome to join us at dinner. We can have guests whenever we want, and the assumption is always that the new arrival's family will eat with them the first night."

"Oh!" Sarah turned around and Hunkman's expression went back to pleasant and professional. "Well, I don't want to be a bother."

"Food's good. Well, you know, for institutional food it's amazing. For regular people food it's good."

Hunkman smiled again. "And you won't be a bother. I can guarantee that Missus Wilson has assumed you'd be eating with your grandfather."

On cue, Samuel came out. He'd indeed freshened up. Clearly personal care was a big deal for him, because he'd changed his shirt and shoes, combed his hair, and put on cologne. It was really a pity he was straight, because he was just what Joseph was looking for. Then again, I was open to being in a new relationship, even if he wasn't young enough for me, so better luck next time to Joseph and hot damn for me.

Introductions were made, then we headed for the dining room. All the group and general rooms were on the ground floor. As with the residential floors, the ground floor was divided into twelfths. Because the haunts liked to start at the top and work down, the wards on this floor had the highest numbers, not the lowest. This ensured that most of us didn't worry about what numbers things were and just sort of went on landmarks. However, because Sarah was along, the confusing explanation was made.

The T intersection was where the elevators, general lobby area, and main entrance were. While we didn't share this with Sarah, the main intersection area tended to be a haunts-free hangout zone. Not that they didn't pass through this area, on any and every floor. They did. But they didn't stay there. However, most visitors felt funny if they were in this section after dark. Dead people walking through you tended to freak folks out, apparently.

It wasn't totally dark out yet, so when Sarah's cell phone rang and she stopped right in the middle of the lobby to answer it, I didn't think we needed to rush her.

However, I was perfectly happy to wait for her because that meant I could hear at least her side of the conversation. Hey, haunts get old hat after you've known them for a while, but eavesdropping on the young folks never gets boring.

"No," Sarah said quietly. "I'm going to stay with Granddad and have dinner. No, I told you I'd stay as long as I could. You were invited to come with us. Not my fault you chose to stay home and watch the game with your friends."

She rolled her eyes. "Really? Because there are *so* many options in a retirement home." Her eyes flicked to Hunkman, then quickly away. "Anyway, I'll be back sometime later. No, I don't know when. Why does it matter anyway? You got what you wanted."

Sarah's eyes narrowed. "You know, my grandfather's here, making friends, and I'm going to stay with him until I feel like leaving. You've gotten what you wanted. I'll talk to you later." She hung up, dropped her phone back into her purse, and put on a fake smile. "That was Norman,"

"Missing you, is he?" Samuel asked mildly.

Sarah shrugged. "So he claims." She put her arm through Samuel's. "But I'm going to have dinner with my Granddad, so he can just fend for himself."

Having been around the dating block many more times than once, as well as being married three times, it wasn't hard to note that this conversation wasn't in keeping with the "happily engaged and can't wait for the wedding" mentality I'd have expected. Clearly there were problems in Sarah's paradise.

Hunkman walked us in, then went to get some of the others. I never needed an escort, but Hunkman escorted me to dinner anyway, just because we liked each other. Others, however, did need assistance, and that was the main thing the orderlies did during the dinner hours.

The Home had options for both large dining and small. We'd chosen the small dining room, meaning it was set up like a typical cafeteria, so we walked through, got our food, then sat at a small table for four. Joseph, clearly hoping that Samuel was open to expanding his horizons in his old age, joined us.

"So, your young man, Norman, what does he do?" Joseph asked Sarah as soon as we all were seated. Or maybe Joseph had picked up something when Samuel and I weren't around and was as suspicious and interested in Sarah's love life as I was.

"He's in insurance," Sarah said.

"How interesting," Joseph replied politely.

"Is it?" I found it hard to believe that insurance was ever interesting.

Sarah shrugged. "To him, I guess."

"He's done quite well for himself," Samuel said. "Should be able to take good care of Sarah."

Sarah looked uncomfortable and we switched the conversation to the Home and its history. Hunkman came over to check on us. Sarah visibly perked up in his presence, as did Joseph and I. Samuel seemed the same. It was final – he was straight and not open to experimentation.

Sarah tore herself away from her grandfather after dinner. We walked her to her car and Samuel waved until she was out of sight. Joseph and I looked at each other. "You taking the lead?" he asked me quietly.

I nodded. "So, Samuel, why, exactly, are you here instead of with your granddaughter, where both of you clearly would prefer you to be?"

He turned around and for the first time looked like an old man. "Norman wants them to start life fresh. I'm well past my freshness date."

"Pardon me for saying this, but I've heard two conversations your Sarah has had with Norman," Joseph shared. "And she doesn't sound 'in love' when she speaks with him. She sounds…resigned."

Samuel sighed. "She was engaged before, to Reed, a wonderful young man, and they were madly in love."

"What happened?"

"He picked her parents, my son and daughter-in-law, up at the airport on their way home from their twenty-fifth anniversary trip that Sarah, Reed and I had given them. Sarah and I stayed home to decorate the house with all the 'welcome home' signs and so forth." His eyes were bright, even in the light of the entryway. With tears, I was pretty sure.

"And?" Joseph asked gently.

"There was a terrible accident on the freeway. They were a part of it. The police insist they all died instantly, but the coroner's report indicated they probably suffered."

"How long ago?"

"Three years." Samuel cleared his throat. "Sarah's not cared about romantic love since then. Norman fits a model she's chosen – successful, upwardly mobile, good lineage – and that's what she's focused on now."

"She doesn't strike me as that rigid a person."

Samuel shrugged. "She wasn't growing up. But now? Now I don't know. She let so much of herself die along with them, and what can I say to make it better? Nothing I've tried has worked, and when you get right down to it, I just want someone who will be able to take care of her when I'm gone. Norman will be that someone, and even though he doesn't want me underfoot, I care more that he'll be there for Sarah when I'm gone."

I refrained from saying that anyone who was trying to get Sarah's beloved grandfather locked away so he wouldn't be underfoot was someone who couldn't care less about Sarah.

The three of us went back inside and headed for the elevators. We left Joseph on the fourth floor. "How full is our section?" Samuel asked as we reached our floor.

"We're the only ones in Section Twelve right now."

"Why is that?"

"We're a very…active…Ward."

"You said Ward, not Section."

"Yes. Good catch. As you so cleverly figured out, this place used to be divided into wards. And at night, it turns back into a hospital."

"Really?" The sadness that he'd had since Sarah had left was replaced by curiosity. Good. Curious folks tended to survive well here.

"Yes indeed. I'll come get you at the witching hour."

"Midnight?"

"No. Around here, the witching hour is whenever it's fully dark out. So it changes daily, in that sense. Should be in about an hour."

"Should I watch the clock so I don't fall asleep and miss it?"

I snorted. "No. Believe me, you'll know when the festivities start."

Tonight's full dark was, apparently, 9:37, an hour after the official end of what the official folks called Civil Twilight. You learned a lot living here, including when the sun rose and set every day.

I heard them before I saw them. But that tended to be the way it was with babies.

Yes, Ward 12 had been the delivery section back in the old days of this place's heyday. Unfortunately, babies didn't all live through childbirth or their first few days. Neither did all their mothers.

Hunkman knocked on my door at 9:38. "Sorry I'm late," he said as he came inside. "Had to settle Mister Newman in."

Newman was going to die soon and we all knew it. He knew it, too. And, because he'd lived here a long time, he wanted to choose his Ward, so he'd get to hang out with his favorite haunts during, as the ghosts called it, the "off hours". Newman fancied the Emergency Ward, God alone knew why, but he said it was because everyone in it had died in some exciting way. The Emergency Ward had been on the ground floor in the old days. So, every night, Hunkman had to move Newman to what was now the Rec Room. Some nights this took a little longer than others.

"Not to worry, nothing's started yet. We should get Samuel, though. He's curious."

Hunkman nodded. "Be interesting to see if he can handle it here." He trotted off and was back quickly with Samuel, who was in pajamas, a nice robe, and expensive slippers, looking a lot like Hugh Hefner had decades ago.

"You haven't changed for bed," Samuel pointed out.

"Can't slip anything past you. No, I tend to wait until later to go to bed."

Samuel nodded. "I can understand why. The babies...do they ever stop crying?"

"Yes." I cleared my throat. "How's your singing voice?"

Samuel gaped at me while Hunkman chuckled. "I – fair, I suppose."

"Well, get ready. I've got everyone trained. Five songs, and all's well."

"Five?" Samuel asked weakly.

"Five," Hunkman said firmly. "They know all the words, so if you don't, Mattie has the music and lyrics for you to follow."

"And little ones love repetition. We're doing *Mockingbird*."

Samuel nodded. "That's a good lullaby. I know it, I'm sure, but it might be good to look at what lyrics you use." I'd been prepared and handed him the printout. "What others?" he asked after he gave it a quick scan.

Hunkman and I exchanged the "newbies" glance. "No other. Repetition. Five full versions of Mockingbird. Let's see if you're a tenor, baritone or bass."

He gaped at us. "We change the song selections now and then," Hunkman said with a grin. "But they have their favorites."

Samuel managed to close his mouth. "What about the...ladies?" He was looking at the wall that separated our rooms. Mothers were wandering back and forth.

"Oh, they're just checking you out like all the living tenants did earlier. They'll settle down and relax once the babies are quieted."

Samuel stared at us for a long moment, then he laughed. "Active Seniors indeed."

I grinned. "Yes, that title works on all sorts of levels, doesn't it?"

Happily, Samuel was a tenor. We hadn't had a tenor for a while and though Hunkman had a lovely baritone, it was always nice to have a change. I held out hope we'd score a bass one day, but so far, hadn't happened. *Swing Low, Sweet Chariot* just wasn't the same without someone singing deep and low.

Five renditions of *Mockingbird* done, we all had a nice long drink of water. "Okay, everyone. Time for quiet play and such. We're going to introduce Samuel around."

The women waved. Each female ghost in this section had at least one baby, some had more. They hadn't all died along with their children, but they'd died while the mothering instinct was at its height, so they'd all taken on babies.

Samuel looked troubled as we walked through the hall. "Why are there so many of them here? I thought babies went directly to Heaven."

"We don't know," Hunkman said. "Though Mattie has a theory."

"I think the presence of a mother held them. Then, as more died, more were held, if you will."

"But…they're missing out."

"On what?"

"Heaven. The afterlife."

"Either they aren't getting in or they're enjoying their time here."

"The psychic energy is particularly strong in this facility," Hunkman explained. "They aren't alone. Our haunts aren't restricted to their Wards, it's just where they sleep during the daytime and wake up, if you will."

"Then they visit, just like we are."

Samuel shook his head. "I don't understand why they stay."

"Oh, some for unfinished business. Some to have hope of keeping tabs on their loved ones. And over time, well, they belong here. It's home."

We crossed into Ward Eleven. "Hi Grandma Mattie!" Several haunts floated out of their rooms and came along with us. George was their spokesman, mostly because he'd been the eldest when he died. "Who's the new arrival?"

"This is Samuel, George."

"They're all children," said new arrival shared. He sounded upset. Well, that was normal. I'd been one of the few who'd caught on right away. It was one of the reasons Hunkman liked me.

"Yes, this is the Children's Wing."

"He's only ten."

"I was eleven when I passed," George said. "It's okay, Samuel. There's no pain anymore and all my friends are here." He waved his hand to indicate the many other young-looking haunts.

"We're all older than Mattie," Delilah said, smiling so her dimples would show well. "And she's really old."

"Careful, I know how to smack your little ghost butt."

Delilah giggled. "Have to catch me first!" She ran off through the floor, heading downstairs. The other children followed her. Other than George.

Samuel cleared his throat. "I'm sixty-seven. Ah, how many years young are you, Mattie?"

"How many do you think? Be honest, I'm hard to offend."

He gave me an appraising look. "Honestly? I think you're younger than me. Sixty-five, maybe?"

Hunkman laughed softly and George laughed loudly while I snorted. I enjoyed snorting, so it was nice of Samuel to afford me so many opportunities. "I'm eighty-two."

"What?!" Samuel shook his head. "There's no way."

"My family looks like delicate flowers but we're a hearty, long-lived breed. And…"

"And?" Samuel prompted.

Might as well tell him. "If you survive here, well...you *really* survive here."

"I don't follow you."

"We've determined that the psychic energy helps to elongate life," Hunkman said. "Missus Wilson isn't aware of it and wouldn't believe it even if we told her. And it doesn't work for everyone. Longevity is passed on to those who are of the right psychic bent. We won't know if you're one or not for a while."

Samuel was quiet for a few seconds. "Huh. Well, having seen and interacted with ghosts, no offence to you, George, I suppose I can make the leap."

"None taken," George said cheerfully. "We don't mind being called ghosts, or haunts, or whatever. Just don't call us ghouls, because we're not."

"Duly noted. But, Mattie, three husbands or not, how do you continue to pay to live here if you're here so much longer than...might be expected?" Samuel asked carefully.

"You're taking this all very well. I'm pleased. And you pay for it as long as your money holds out, just like anywhere else. It's got the usual government subsidies and the like." I chose not to mention that some of our haunts weren't restricted to this location. Or, rather, they'd learned how to filter out through the internet. And at the Home, we took care of our own.

"Don't worry, Samuel," George said. "If you want to stay here forever, you can. If you want to move on when you die, you can. It's just...we don't know what's really out there. And this was a hospital, sure, but only a few choose to keep their problems with them. You just stay away from Downstairs at night and you'll be fine."

"Come on, slowpoke!" Delilah's head popped up from the floor. "Sister Mary Margaret's going to do story time!"

Delilah's head disappeared again and George followed. We three were alone in the hallway again.

"Let's head downstairs," Hunkman said. "We're a little late for the rounds."

"I thought we weren't supposed to go downstairs," Samuel said.

"We aren't going where George meant. There's downstairs, and then there's Downstairs with a capital D. George means the capital D – the two lower levels. You shouldn't go down there at night, potentially ever, but not without me or Hunkman or one of the more experienced residents or orderlies."

"Why not?" Samuel asked as we got onto the elevator, along with the medical personnel who'd died on duty. They liked to take the elevators because it made them feel more solid, or so they said. I figured they just enjoyed the "feeling" of weightlessness being on an elevator provided. Or they liked to really scrunch up close to the living. Or both.

"Because this hospital's psych ward was underground."

Over the course of the week, Samuel met the rest of the residents, living and ghostly. Sarah visited him every day, so she knew all the living residents as well, though she'd missed out on the haunts so far. It was clear she wasn't happy about Samuel's moving in, though she got along with all of us, Hunkman especially.

But she wasn't coming to flirt, sadly. She was coming to be with her grandfather.

Samuel had the best record for familial attendance of any new resident, ever, and that included the ones whose families didn't really want said resident to move into Happy Acres. Sarah gave the impression of being willing to come by every day for the rest of Samuel's life. While this was lovely and to be wished for every senior in any home anywhere, it was taking love and loyalty to an extreme that seemed just a tad unnatural.

Sarah herself was a lovely girl, smart, pretty, and, when not discussing wedding plans or her intended, vivacious. She possessed an actual sense of humor as well as kindness and compassion, though she hid the humorous side a lot. She'd been career-oriented before her great loss, but now just seemed focused on going through the motions in regard to everything other than Samuel.

Joseph and I both spent some effort to get the full Norman story out of her. We were rewarded with the firm conviction that Sarah was making a horrible life decision based out of grief and fear. Norman would probably make some woman a good husband, but Sarah wasn't going to be that woman. He was jealous, but in a controlling way. In fact, the main word for Norman was "controlling".

But Sarah wasn't my only concern. I had a long-standing concern I kept an eye on. Hunkman was acting a little off, and I was pretty sure it was because of Sarah.

"So," I said as he came to gather us for dinner the anniversary of Samuel's first week with us. "You going to make a move?"

"On who?" Hunkman asked mildly.

"On Sarah. She's interested, trust me as a woman, and she needs someone to get her away from her odious fiancé."

Hunkman's eyes shown for a moment. But then the light died and he shook his head. "I'm taken. You know that."

I did. I was about the most open person you could ask for, but I drew the line at someone having a true romantic relationship with a ghost, despite the fact that *The Ghost and Mrs. Muir* was a Home favorite. I drew a harsher line when said ghost resided Downstairs. And that only for roughly three days a month. Three special days.

Hunkman had fallen in love with the wrong girl from the wrong time. But until Sarah had shown up, I hadn't found a viable alternative. Now, it might be possible to get a double and save two people from their own bad romantic choices.

Clearly it was time to plot. Which was fine with me, because I was a world-class plotter.

It was the end of Samuel's second week. He, Sarah and I were in the dining room at a larger table for eight, with Joseph, Janice, Trudy, Thomas, and, sadly, Betsy. Betsy was doing her best to flirt with Samuel, who was either clueless or uninterested, because he wasn't catching it at all. He was also seated between me and Sarah, so Betsy didn't have a lot of options other than batting her eyelashes, which she did. Endlessly.

"Bets, do you have something in your eyes?" It was a cheap shot, but still satisfying.

She glared at me. "Not at all."

"Ah. Just had to use the special cataract drops today, then, huh?" I didn't give Betsy a chance to reply. Instead I looked at Sarah. "So, when are you going to bring your Norman by to meet all of us?"

"Oh, I don't know." Sarah looked slightly trapped. No problem, I wanted her trapped, but trapped with the right guy.

"Are you ashamed of us?" Joseph, who was in on my plot, asked. Hey, it always helped to have a wingman. And it had given me an extra person to help with my questioning of our haunts in the Wards that had either been or seen a lot of women who'd "bumped into door knobs" in their days.

"Oh, no! Of course not." Sarah looked to Samuel for help.

"I think it would be nice for Norman to meet everyone," Samuel said in that noncommittal way that indicates the speaker would like to ensure no one ends up mad at him.

"Then I'll make it happen," Sarah said brightly. I knew it was faked, but she did a good job with the faking. I had a feeling she faked Norman out regularly.

"Great, how about tomorrow night?"

"I - I'll check." Sarah pulled her phone out and spent much of the rest of the meal texting. I assumed Norman wanted to come visit the Home only slightly more than he wanted a root canal.

Dessert arrived with no confirmation from Norman. "Tapioca again. What were the odds?"

"Oh, this has the cinnamon on top, just like you like it, Mattie," Samuel said with a laugh.

Interesting. We'd had tapioca eight times so far, and only one time had there been cinnamon on top. So, he was observant. At least in terms of my likes and dislikes. Of course, he was technically almost twenty years too young for me, and that meant he really wasn't young enough. But, he truly was a looker. Depending on how things went, I might have to make an exception.

"Norman can't come tomorrow, or the day after, but he can come the day after that," Sarah announced with relief. "Will that work?"

Two, three, or even four nights from now were going to be bad for Hunkman. But that might end up for the best. Or the worst. Prognostication wasn't actually a ghostly trait, so we didn't get an edge up from our special residents on knowing the future. They were great with the past, however.

My extra two seconds of silence were filled by Betsy. "It'll be perfect, I'm sure. Hopefully your young man will stay for dinner."

"Yes, that's the plan," Sarah said.

"Then it's settled." Betsy looked exceedingly smug, as if she'd set the whole thing up. But she could take the credit for Norman's coming to visit.

It would make it easier for her to take the blame for anything that went wrong when he was here.

"This Norman might be a fine young man," Joseph said as we sunned ourselves. Well, as we sat there, fully clothed, under an umbrella so as to avoid the risk of melanoma, and let the sun's heat warm us indirectly.

"He might be, and if he is, then we just need to determine why Sarah's not in love with him."

"You think there's more going on, don't you?"

I shrugged. "I've known Samuel for a little over two weeks and he and I have a far more cozy relationship than it seems his granddaughter has with the man she's going to marry."

"He's worried about it, too."

"Did he tell you so, man to man?"

"No. But I can tell by his expression when he thinks no one's looking at him."

"And yet you saw said expression."

"You're hilarious. As if I didn't spend the majority of my life looking at other men without them knowing?"

"Good point." I patted his hand. "Someone right will come for you soon. I'm sure of it."

"There are worse things than spending your later years in a place like this, surrounded by friends and interesting people, both alive and dead. So I don't need your pity," he added with a laugh.

"No pity from me, mister. Not for you."

"Right. We need to save our pity for those who need it." Joseph cleared his throat. "Jason...do you think you can get him interested in Sarah?"

"Hunkman's already interested in her. Don't you see how he looks at her?"

"Yes, I do. And then I see him look down, and when he looks back up, he has that look. The look *she* gave him." He didn't mean Sarah, and I knew it. "You know she won't let him go. And if she doesn't let him go, then Sarah has no chance, even if she were to throw herself at Jason."

Joseph was right, and he didn't need me to provide confirmation. I sighed and contemplated my options. They weren't plentiful.

"There's nothing for it. I'm going to have to go Downstairs. Tonight."

I waited for the gasp of horror, or for Joseph to demand that I not be foolhardy, to beg me to think of the consequences. "I agree."

"That's it? You agree?"

He chuckled. "You're the only one who's ever frightened her. You know her weakness."

"True enough. I just hope I can exploit it."

"It's you, Mattie. Of course you can exploit it. So, you going to keep Samuel or toss him back into the sea?"

"Oh, jury's still out on that one. He's really not young enough for me."

It was the first night of the full moon. Tomorrow, when the moon would be honestly full, was when Norman was coming to dinner. But I needed to get a lay of the land, so to speak.

Hunkman joined me and Samuel at 9:37 sharp for our regular sing along with the little ones. Joseph joined us, too, as did Trudy and Janice, walker and all.

One of the things most people think they know about ghosts is that they have to stay the age they were when they died. This was true, in a sense. No ghost can make its form "age" past the age of their death. However, ghosts can revert to a younger form if they want to. They can go back and forth, though most picked the age when they felt the most fit and attractive and stuck with it.

While their bodies, so to speak, were limited, their minds were not. Their minds could and did move forward. So a ghost who's been dead a hundred years has whatever earthly experiences to draw from, in addition to all the ghostly experiences once dead.

For the ghost children like George and Delilah, this meant they tended to act like kids, because that's what their forms were, but they had decades of mental experiences, meaning they were farther along than most of the Home's residents.

Most of the residents could handle the older ghosts, even the kids, because they could and did interact with us for the most part like adults or children of the age of intelligent communication. But for whatever reason, the babies never aged in their minds. And after a while that freaked everyone out. Other than me. But then again, I understood why they chose to stay infants, and why the mothers chose to let them. I also understood the benefits of their choices better than anyone else.

So it was a sacrifice for the others to come for the sing-along time, but Joseph and I had impressed the need upon them, and they were only going to have to do it for a couple of nights anyway.

When song time was over Janice, ever the champ, created a problem with her walker, so that Hunkman had to focus his attention on fixing it. Joseph and Trudy, meanwhile, distracted Samuel by getting into a conversation with some of the ghost mothers about what the next lullaby selection should be and if it should be sooner as opposed to later.

I slipped out and walked quickly down the hall. George joined me. "Grandma Mattie, what are you doing?"

"Going Downstairs."

"Do you want company?"

Really? Yet another one who didn't even offer a mention of the danger or a protest that I shouldn't meddle with things man or woman should not wont of? Fine. They knew I'd just snort at them, and not everyone loved my snorting like I did.

"Would love it, but I don't know that it's a good idea. I need to have a chat with herself."

"I don't envy you." George joined me in the elevator.

I hit the button for B1. I really hoped I wouldn't have to go down to B2. "Thanks. It's got to be done."

"She won't give him up."

"She might. If she has something better."

"Better than Hunkman?"

"Better in her viewpoint."

"Call if you need me or the others. Mister Newman's hosting a bon voyage party, so most of us will be closer than normal to Downstairs."

"He thinks he's going that soon?"

"He says tomorrow," George said as he exited the elevator at the ground floor. "So we'll see."

I considered all my options as the elevator went downward. There was a pinging sound and then the doors opened.

"Here we go again," I said to no one in particular.

Ghosts don't normally have a smell unless they died in some horrible way that requires either revenge or atonement.

Or if they really hated you and wanted you to have to smell something bad for a while.

Our standard haunts sometimes brought out their favorite scents for special occasions – deaths, usually, which they looked at as welcoming an old friend to the joys of walking through walls.

Downstairs was different. The first thing that hit you when you came down here after real dark was that it stank to high heaven. These ghosts hated everyone and wanted anyone visiting to know so.

I'd told Samuel that the dead couldn't hurt you. This was mostly true. But the ghosts Downstairs had the best chance, and the most motivation, to harm the living. Her especially.

We didn't use or think her name because her name gave her power. She'd been a grande dame of the stage and silver screen both in her day, adored by millions, and they'd chanted her name. She loved her name – seeing it in lights, in the film credits, but especially hearing it come from someone else's lips.

She had talents beyond those required of actresses, and she'd used them to enhance her fame and her allure. Women wanted to be her and men wanted to be with her and all that gave her more power.

Then she'd gotten a little older and latched onto some unpopular ideas, including the idea of telling people about her true powers. Her handlers had declared her insane, stolen her fortune, and locked her down here in the psych ward. Horrible things had happened to her down here. And for what she'd gone through, I did pity her.

I pitied all of them. The psych ward had been run by both the viciously psychotic and the humane, depending on the era. But if you're batshit crazy, you may not be able to recognize kindness. And if you were sent here for things like being homosexual or having the wrong political beliefs or wanting equal treatment under the law, or being an actual magic-wielding witch, you were going to be frightened and angry. Very, very angry.

There were only angry, insane haunts Downstairs. The ones who'd retained their sanity or humanity had fled at the moments of their death. They'd gone where George and the others feared to tread, because the vast unknown was better than what they'd lived through.

But only one of them had made a deal with the Devil to exact her revenge.

Of course, she said it was the Devil, but who knew? I didn't ascribe to the idea that witchcraft was the Devil's work, for a variety of reasons, common sense being first and foremost. Everyone had talents, and some people's talents involved doing things others felt were supernatural. What we did know for sure was that she'd gotten more power than most ghosts possessed, but the tradeoff was that she could only manifest during the three nights of the full moon.

Everyone in the Home learned fast not to come Downstairs after true dark. But sometimes, you had to. The orderlies in particular. The orderlies knew to come down in pairs or groups and to never separate. And everyone knew never to go Downstairs during the three nights of the full moon. But sometimes, it couldn't be avoided.

That's how she'd found Hunkman. We'd had a pipe break and he'd had to come down here to fix it before the Home and all the medical offices flooded. The other orderlies were taking care of residents, so he'd gone Downstairs alone. And come upstairs a changed man.

However, I had protection Hunkman didn't have. Just like I knew things about him, and her, no one else did.

There were a lot of ghosts around me all of a sudden, all screeching, trying to touch me, doing the usual House of Horrors thing. I decided I didn't have time for it.

"Bugger off, all of you. You don't scare me, but I know how to scare you. You don't take off and leave me alone, it's the *Barney* Theme Song at the top of my lungs. And I can do it in the dinosaur's voice, too, so don't try me. And if that doesn't scare all of you, *Pineapple Princess* and the complete set of nineteen-fifties teenaged death rock songs will follow. And we'll finish up with *MacArthur Park.*"

It was amazing, but there was power in horrible music and a threat they all knew I was willing and quite able to follow through on. I was completely alone fast. Well, almost completely alone.

"Hello Matilda." The voice was lovely, clearly projecting from the diaphragm. "So good of you to pay me a visit."

It sounded like she was behind me, but I didn't bother to turn around. Instead I kept on, heading for what had, back in the day, been the room where they did the shock treatments. "How's it going?"

She appeared in front of me. Naturally, she looked young, and terribly beautiful. Hourglass figure, pursed lips, wavy blonde hair, large, luminous eyes. She'd paid good attention to how she'd looked in makeup, because she was absolutely ready for her close-up. "You want something."

"Everyone wants something. You, in particular."

"I have all I want." She looked behind me. "My beloved will be here shortly. I expect you to be gone by the time he arrives."

"Yeah, about that. That's not really working for me anymore."

She leaned closer. "You've come to threaten me?"

I walked through her. It wasn't a comfortable feeling, but being old meant I'd had plenty of experiences that felt worse than the sensation of slimy cold going through you for a few seconds.

I entered the shock treatment room. It was actually the woman's restroom now, go figure. She didn't follow. I turned around. "I know what will destroy you."

She laughed, and it tinkled on the air. "Hardly. Your musical threats don't bother me."

"I have other threats to share with you. See, we have this amazing thing called film preservation. It's crazy what the kids these days are coming up with. And, you'll be pleased to know that your entire filmography has made it onto discs, in the full Criterion Collection special set."

"The world can see me again?" Her eyes burned. "Show me."

"Oh, no. Let's remember why I'm here. You need to break up, nicely, with Jason, without harming him in either mind, soul, body, or longevity. Tonight. Or tomorrow night, I'll bring the full collection down here. And play all your films."

"Why would that frighten *me*?"

The advantage of spending lots of time with ghosts was that you could learn a lot from them. I'd learned that not only people but things lasted beyond their time of destruction, especially things that had strong human emotions connected to them. And no emotions were stronger than the combination of fear, hatred, and pain.

I concentrated. Yes, I could just see them. I reached out and took the ghostly shock pads in my hands. "As I play your films, I'll use these on the images of you. Each frame will get shocked. Until the disc that contains the movie is destroyed."

She shook. "You wouldn't dare."

"Try me. I'm pretty sure you'll feel every shock."

Her expression told me that she was sure she would. "I'll destroy you!"

"Oh yeah? Come into the room and say that."

"Try to leave, and I will have everyone here rend you."

I snorted. One of my best, at least if her flinch was any indication. "First off, Jason's about to come down, and if you hurt me in front of him, he'll despise you and leave you anyway. Secondly, I could just wait you out. Daylight's not *that* far off and I have no issues with sleeping sitting up on occasion, and if *you're* not brave enough to come in here, I know for fact that none of the others are, either. And lastly, I may have another guy for you, anyway."

She cocked her head. "You offer me someone to replace my beloved? Why?"

"Because I think he might deserve you. I'll know for sure tomorrow."

I heard the ping of the elevator. Damn, Hunkman was on the floor.

"Then come back with him tomorrow. I will not release my beloved tonight. Either it will be our last night together or you and I will fight to the death."

I didn't want to do any of this with Hunkman watching. "Fine. But know that I'll win."

"And why is that?"

I smiled as I walked out of the bathroom. "Because I'm smarter than you."

Hunkman saw me. "Mattie, what are you doing down here?"

"Looking for something."

He shook his head. "Come on, I'm getting you back upstairs."

We got into the elevator. There were two of us, only. She'd stayed out of his sight. Good.

We got upstairs and I decided it was time to pull out the big guns. I clutched my chest. "Jason...I feel odd."

His face drained of color. "You...you haven't called me Jason since I started working here."

"I know," I gasped. "I need to lie down."

He picked me up and carried me to my room. As soon as he had me lying down he sent a couple of the ghosts to ask another orderly to come up. Hunkman took my pulse, checked my heart, the whole deal.

"You seem okay," he said uncertainly.

"I'd feel better if you stayed with me tonight. Just in case." This wasn't a lie. If he was here, he wasn't going to be with her, and that would definitely make me feel better.

He looked down, then back up at me. "Okay."

Hunkman watched over me all night. Any time it appeared that he might think I was safely asleep I ensured I did the moan and toss thing and he stayed put.

Morning came, and I declared that I felt better. Hunkman insisted on taking me down for tests. Shockingly, the doctors didn't find anything wrong with me. I did admit to being a little tired which was true because I hadn't actually slept all night.

I took a nap while Hunkman went off shift and home to sleep. Samuel and Joseph checked in on me, Joseph to ensure that our plot was still going strong, Samuel because he was deeply concerned. Which was very sweet.

I took a nice long nap and was up in time for the second lunch shift at 1. Samuel was waiting for me and offered to bring up a tray, but I didn't want to carry on the Delicate Flower charade any longer. I had work to do.

Lunch was pleasant, with everyone expressing concerns over my health, other than Betsy, who took the opportunity to comment snidely on my advancing years. I let her have her moment. It wasn't fun to spar with someone if they never managed to hit you a little; if they couldn't fight back that made you a bully and them a victim. Betsy was a lot of things, but, happily, victim wasn't one of them.

The afternoon dragged on, always the way when you're anticipating something. But it gave me time to have a nice, long chat with Mr. Newman, about his life and his afterlife goals.

Sarah and Norman arrived around 6. He was nice enough looking, though older than I'd expected. Sarah was in her mid-twenties, but Norman was in his late thirties. I didn't have too much of an issue with age differences, but only when the rest of the relationship worked.

Introductions were made. To everyone. They caught the first dinner set as they were leaving the dining room and the rest of us as we were heading towards it.

Sarah hugged me and gave me the DVD I'd asked her to pick up. "Granddad said you had a bad night last night."

"Fit as a fiddle, now." I held up the DVD. "This'll be all I need to feel a hundred percent." I was wearing a sweater with large pockets and I slid the DVD into one of them.

She nodded. "I'm happy to get you anything you need, Mattie. Granddad said Jason found you and stayed with you all night."

Norman had been mid-introduction with Thomas, but his head swiveled towards us just like a snake going after prey. "Who's Jason?"

"The Chief Nurse, I told you about him," Sarah said, carefully not making eye contact with Norman.

Whose eyes narrowed. "What kind of a guy goes in for being a nurse instead of a doctor?" Nice to see Norman carried some clearly outdated ideas. Nice in the sense that the chances of me feeling guilty for what I was going to do were moving to the slim side.

"Someone who knows his true calling," Sarah said, just a tad defensively.

"Right." Norman shoved a smile onto his face. "You must be Sammy's new girlfriend."

I saw Samuel start to blush. He'd never once suggested any of us call him Sammy, Sam, or any other nickname, and I doubted he'd offered that nickname to Norman. Plus, we hadn't had a date. This meant either that Sarah was assuming, or Samuel had told her he liked me and she'd let it slip to

Norman. My guilt levels went to slim-to-none, but I did have to be sure. And stall things out for several hours.

"Oh, Samuel hasn't made an official love connection that any of us know of," Betsy said, fluttering her eyelashes at Samuel and Norman both. I hated to admit it, but her timing was good.

"True enough. So, let's have dinner, so we all get to know Norman better."

In addition to tables for four and eight, there were also longer cafeteria-type tables in the larger dining room for twelve and sixteen. I headed us for one of the twelve-seaters and ensured that Norman got seated in the middle, with his back to a wall. It was going to take a lot for him to get out easily, especially since Janice and her walker were at one end and Joseph was at the other.

I was purposely slow to sit down, so Betsy claimed the open seat next to Samuel. Sarah, of course, was on his other side, with Norman next to her. I took the seat opposite Norman.

There were a variety of questions and answers, personality traits, and tells Joseph and I had gleaned from the haunts who'd been victims of or around domestic violence which would help us determine if Norman fell into this group. Controlling nature was at the top of the list, along with unreasonable jealousy, and overreactions to minor or perceived threats.

We all chatted and asked questions. Norman seemed normal, pun intended, but the real test had come on shift a little late, due to having to take care of me the night before.

As we were finishing dinner, Sarah looked behind me and her eyes lit up. It didn't take genius to guess that Hunkman had come into the dining room. Norman's reaction, however, was what I was interested in.

He spotted Hunkman, too, and immediately looked at Sarah. "Who's that?"

"Jason Helkman, the Head Nurse."

"Head Orderly as far as the management is concerned," Hunkman said with a gleaming smile as he joined us. "You must be Norman. Sarah's told me a lot about you."

"Has she? She hasn't told me much about you."

Hunkman laughed. "Why would she?" He put his hand on my shoulder. "How are you doing tonight, Mattie?"

"Oh, much better, dear."

Hunkman stared at me. I called him dear about as often as I called him Jason. "I'm going to check on the others, Mister Newman in particular, and then I'm going to be keeping an eye on you, young lady." He nodded to Norman. "Nice to meet you."

Norman waited until Hunkman was out of hearing range. "Just what have you said about me?" he asked Sarah, voice icy.

"That we're getting married, what you do, you know, the usual things you tell people," Sarah replied. "What's wrong with you?"

"Nothing." It was clear from Norman's tone and expression that he was lying.

"I think someone's jealous," Betsy said with a giggle. It was amazing, the exact thing I wanted someone to say, and she popped out with it. I sincerely hoped I wasn't going to have to start liking her.

Sarah put her hand onto Norman's. "There's no reason. I'm marrying you."

Norman snatched his hand away. "We'll talk about it later. In private."

Joseph and I exchanged a look. Even though he was at the end of the table, he hadn't missed anything. He nodded. So I had Joseph's go-ahead confirmation.

Time to roll the plot and let the best man win.

We'd figured Norman was going to want to leave right after dinner and had planned accordingly.

"You can't deny the wishes of a dying man," Joseph said as Norman tried to give another reason why he and Sarah needed to take off.

"Mister Newman's sure he's going to die tonight," I said. "He wants to see all of us, and he's been so keen to meet you, Norman."

"Why?" Norman asked bluntly.

But I was prepared. "We're all happy to have Samuel with us, and we all love Sarah. Naturally we've all been wanting to meet her intended. And Mister Newman's convinced he won't see tomorrow, so it's really rather imperative we go visit him now."

Norman sputtered some protests, but Sarah shook her head. "No, Mister Newman's a sweetheart and we're not going to disappoint him. Besides, we took my car, so you're not going anywhere."

Norman actually reached for her purse, presumably to grab her keys out of it. But Sarah moved it deftly out of his reach. "You're being very rude," she said in a low voice. "Stop it."

He shot her a look that said volumes, all of them badly written with a lot of nasty inside. "Fine. If I don't close any sales calls tomorrow, we'll know whose fault it is."

"Really? A young man such as yourself has to be in bed by eight in the evening?" I clucked. "Sarah didn't tell us you were ill."

Norman shot me a look that said he didn't find this funny. It was official – I really couldn't stand him and he'd marry Sarah over my dead body. Well, not over mine, per se, but a dead body or two were definitely going to be involved, and soon.

But first, Newman had some 'splainin' to do.

We ensured that Norman was surrounded as we headed to the Rec Room, so he couldn't make a break for it.

Newman was there, in all his dying soon glory. For a man determined to kick the bucket, he still looked remarkably alive. Of course, that figured into my overall plot, so I was good with it.

Norman was politely shoed right up next to Newman and surrounded by a lot of residents. I remained near the door. I needed to keep an eye on Hunkman and be able to leave the room without anyone noticing.

Newman was a garrulous man and he loved an audience. It helped that he'd been an actor in his younger days. He told story after story, including Norman or Sarah in some way so they couldn't escape without having to announce they were leaving to everyone in the room.

To his credit, Norman let this go on for an hour or so before he tried to leave. Newman was having none of it, and the rest of the group didn't take Norman's excuses either.

It got later, Newman continued on, and then true dark came. I knew without looking at a clock because the haunts arrived.

The emergency room haunts liked to spend their first minutes reenacting their deaths, mostly because they felt it was traditional and demanded of them. Considering Newman was their biggest fan, they were probably right.

So, while Newman talked, there were multiple death scenes going on before us. I'd seen them all by now, but it was interesting to see them all happening at once, so to speak.

Sarah was staring around the room, eyes wide. George and Delilah showed up, smiled at her, and settled next to her. Samuel took her hand and patted it as the rest of Happy Acres' haunts arrived right after them, even the babies, who were all crying, albeit quietly.

The room was filled to capacity in the first place, so the ghostly guests had to float above to keep from walking through every person, though Norman was walked through by many of them. I got the signals I was expecting from the ghosts who'd gone through him – Norman wasn't a nice person at all.

Joseph and Janice quietly distracted Hunkman and I slipped out of the room and trotted to the elevator. Made sure no one had followed me, and headed down to B1.

The ping announced my arrival. As expected, she was waiting for me. "How did you keep him away from me last night?"

"I told you, I'm smarter than you. I could remove Jason from your control myself, there just hasn't been a good option for him until now. However, I'm not without empathy, so I'm going to offer you a very viable alternative. If you agree and help me, you'll be able to keep him with you, forever. Company all the time, not just during the nights of the full moon."

"Whatever you offer will not be as worthy as Jason."

"Well, that's true enough. But he's someone you're going to enjoy, I think. He strikes me as your type."

She focused and looked up. "He is…unpleasant."

"True enough. So none of us are going to care what you do to or with him."

"How will you explain his absence?"

"Well, as to that…"

I headed back upstairs. It was a risky gambit, but nothing ventured, nothing gained. Besides, it would be fun.

Newman was still in full raconteur swing when I returned to the Rec Room. I'd timed it out right, because Hunkman was just starting to edge for the door.

Norman spotted him. "Where are you going?" he asked, interrupting Newman's story about when he was on set with

Paul Newman and a production assistant had mixed them up. This was a good story, making Norman's interruption that much more rude.

"Going to check on things," Hunkman said. He was looking at the babies, and I figured he hoped they'd follow him out of the room so he and I could sing to them and get everything back onto normal schedule.

"What things?" Norman asked. "Everything you should be keeping an eye on is in this room."

Sarah's eyes flashed. "Norman, that was incredibly rude."

He rolled his eyes. "I'm sure. Look, we're leaving. Now." He grabbed Sarah and dragged her towards the door, which meant he was dragging her towards me.

"Do you see anything you weren't expecting here, Norman?"

He looked around, at the living people only. "No. Just a lot of old meat past its expiration date."

So he couldn't see the haunts. There were only a few who couldn't, always because the haunts didn't want to be seen by those people. In Mrs. Wilson's case, it was because they found it funny for her to not know they were here. In Norman's case, I figured it was because they wanted the plot to succeed.

Sarah wrenched out of his grip. "How *dare* you?! You're talking about my Granddad and his friends."

"Get over here," Norman snarled.

Joseph took Sarah's hand and moved her closer to him and Samuel. "I think the young lady will stay right here. Where she's safe."

Norman looked furious, and Hunkman stopped moving towards the door. He headed towards Norman. Those in between them moved away so there was space. "Let me escort you out."

Showing both his temper and his total incomprehension of reality, Norman swung at Hunkman. Hunkman had four inches and at least fifty pounds of muscle on Norman. He blocked the punch, grabbed Norman, and put him into a headlock.

I looked at the DVD I was holding. "It's show time."

The haunts Downstairs were trapped, both physically and psychically and because the other haunts had ensured that the right protections had been put up to keep the dangerous haunts out of the rest of the place. However, a ghost could haunt an object, if that object had significance for them. In her case, her biggest film with her picture and name plastered all over it was definitely significant.

I had to give it to her, she had style. She boiled up out of the DVD, large and imperious. Hunkman saw her and dropped Norman. But not to go to her. He ran and stood in front of Sarah. "Leave her alone."

She looked at me. "See?" I said. "I told you, take the deal."

She nodded. "I accept." She dove into Norman. Literally. She was strong enough to be able to possess someone, for a short time at least.

Joseph and the other haunts started to get everyone else moving out of the room. Her power lifted Norman up into the air, as everyone trundled as fast as they could out of the Rec Room. Hunkman looked up at Norman, then to me. The glamour she'd cast on him that I always saw in his eyes when he was thinking of her was gone.

"Thank you," he said quietly, as he put his arm around Sarah and hustled her out of the room.

In a few moments, there were only me, Newman, the possessed Norman, and all the ghosts of hospital personnel in the room. She set Norman down next to Newman. I put my hands over each of their hearts.

"Doctors, if you'd please perform the transfusion."

The medical haunts surrounded us, doing ghostly things I didn't bother to watch.

Norman's eyes were wide. "What...are you doing?" he gasped out. It was his voice. So she was allowing him to know everything that was happening. A match made in Heaven, or, more likely, Hell.

"I'm giving you a trophy wife you could only dream of. And, in exchange for this, you're giving Newman here a new lease on life."

Norman's body fell onto the floor. "We're done," the head doctor said.

She floated out of Norman's body, Norman's ghost following her, looking confused. He wouldn't be for long. The doctor nodded to her. "He's all yours."

She smiled widely, and it was beautiful and terrible at the same time. She took hold of Norman's ghost. "Come, my beloved. We're going home." She nodded to me. "I have been pleased to do you a favor. Remember that I may need one at some later time."

"I'm sure you will. Now, time to go home." She looked around, and I knew what she was thinking. I waved the DVD. "It's amazingly easy to destroy these things. And to put electrical charges against them."

She nodded and, with a grand leap into the air, flew down through the floor, dragging Norman's now screaming ghost with her.

I bent down. Norman's heart wasn't beating, and his body was already cooling.

"Such a shame," Newman said, as he got out of bed. "Such a young man to have that massive a heart attack."

"So true. Missus Wilson's going to be very upset."

We left the Rec Room. "Norman's had a massive heart attack. I performed CPR, but he didn't revive. I'm sorry."

While a couple of the orderlies raced into the Rec Room and another called 9-1-1, Hunkman comforted Sarah. Samuel seemed like the weight of the world was off his shoulders. Joseph gave me a wink and a thumb's up.

Newman twinkled at me as haunts and the living did what they did most of the time when a death was concerned –

some cried, most went to have a looksee and pretend to be horrified. "So, now that I have more time, what say you and I step out some time? That new fella's a little young for you, Mattie."

Samuel caught me looking at him and flashed a smile. He really did look like Hugh Jackman. Of course, the production assistant had mixed up our Newman with Paul Newman for more reasons than name only.

"Oh, I'm willing to give both of you a go and let the best man win. So, tell me, Newman...are you a tenor, bass, or baritone?"

About the Author

Gini Koch writes the fast, fresh and funny Alien/Katherine "Kitty" Katt series for DAW Books, the Necropolis Enforcement Files, and the Martian Alliance Chronicles. She also has a humor collection, *Random Musings from the Funny Girl*. As G.J. Koch she writes the Alexander Outland series and she's made the most of multiple personality disorder by writing under a variety of other pen names as well, including Anita Ensal, Jemma Chase, A.E. Stanton, and J.C. Koch. She has stories featured in a variety of excellent anthologies, available now and upcoming, writing as Gini Koch, Anita Ensal, and J.C. Koch. She can be reached via her website – **www.ginikoch.com**.

Reach Gini

Her author page: **http://www.ginikoch.com/**
The Blah, Blah, Blah Blog - **http://ginikoch.blogspot.com/**
Twitter - @GiniKoch
Facebook - facebook.com/Gini.Koch
Facebook Fan Page: Hairspray & Rock 'n' Roll –
https://www.facebook.com/GiniKochAuthor
Pinterest – **http://www.pinterest.com/ginikoch/**
The Official Fan Site of the Alien Collective -
http://thealiencollectivevirtualhq.blogspot.com/
    E-mail - gini@ginikoch.com

Gini Koch Writing As...

Anita Ensal
A CUP OF JOE

Anthologies
LOVE AND ROCKETS – *Wanted*
BOONDOCKS FANTASY – *Being Neighborly*
THE BOOK OF EXODI – *The Last Day on Earth*

G.J. Koch
ALEXANDER OUTLAND: SPACE PIRATE

Jemma Chase
THE DISCIPLE AND OTHER STORIES
OF THE PARANORMAL

J.C. Koch
Anthologies
THE MADNESS OF CTHULHU - *Little Lady*
A DARKE PHANTASTIQUE - *Outsiders*
KAIJU RISING: AGE OF MONSTERS -
With Bright Shining Faces

Gini Koch

The Alien/Katherine "Kitty" Katt Series
from DAW Books

Booklist names
TOUCHED BY AN ALIEN
One of the top 10 adult SF/F novels of 2010!

RT Book Reviews Reviewers'
Choice Awards
ALIEN IN THE HOUSE
wins Best Futuristic Romance of 2013!

"If you like your books moving at the speed of sound, with
plenty of action, then look into Gini Koch."
– Fresh Fiction

TOUCHED BY AN ALIEN
978-0-7564-0600-4
Also in audio!

ALIEN TANGO
978-0-7564-0632-5

ALIEN IN CHIEF
Coming December 2015

CAMP ALIEN
Coming May 2016

ALIEN NATION
Coming December 2016

ALIENS ABROAD
Coming May 2017

"Rollicking, sexy fun – science fiction hasn't been this much of a blast since…well, never. Grab on with both hands and enjoy the wild, lusty ride."
– Robert J. Sawyer,
Hugo Award-winning author of *Triggers*

Gini Koch

The Necropolis Enforcement Files Series

"Gini Koch delivers on the humor, mayhem, and mystery
with The Night Beat – this mondo monster noir crackles
with snappy dialogue, great characters, and twists
and turns that will keep you guessing."
– Carolyn Crane,
author of The Disillusionists trilogy

"Do you just LOVE the paranormal world? Historical figures?
Well The Night Beat is an all you can eat buffet of
creatures that bump, thud, poof, sniff, shamble,
or zip in the night!"
– I Smell Sheep

THE NIGHT BEAT
978-1-4776-3138-6

NIGHT MUSIC
Coming 2016

"The fascinating premise of Necroplis City, a place existing
just below Prosaic City (the human location) in another
dimension, that supernatural beings can travel back
and forth between, enhances the story, and
this reviewer hopes to learn more about
the city itself in book two."
– Bitten By Books

Gini Koch
writing as
Jemma Chase

A time-traveling vampire hunter. The search for the hottest place on Earth. A salvage hunter at the edge of the galaxy. A maze that grows more terrifying with each turn. And someone trapped in a deadly game of hide and seek. What do they have in common? Surprises, thrills, twists, romance, and danger, all within different realms of the paranormal. Strange Protection, Hotter Than Hell, Waiting, Amazing, and The Disciple – for the first time, these five short stories, novelettes, and novellas of the paranormal by Gini Koch writing as Jemma Chase are in one collection. These stories will introduce you to dangers and romance lurking around the corner, and show you the secret worlds and creatures just outside of everyday view. So come and enter the paranormal worlds of Jemma Chase. Just remember to bring a map to lead you back to your normal world, because the writer's web is like a maze, and not all mazes have exits.

THE DISCIPLE
AND OTHER STORIES OF
THE PARANORMAL
978-1-5086-5365-3

Gini Koch
writing as
Anita Ensal

When Emily smiles at David, the Chosen One, as if he's a
normal person, his sheltered existence plunges into terror and
deception, forcing him to see that the world might not be as
perfect as he's always believed. If the choice is between love or
perfection, which would you choose?

"Smart, unexpected…A Cup of Joe is solid science fiction with
a big dollop of romance and a tasty twist you won't see
coming."
–Marsheila Rockwell,
author of Dungeons & Dragons Online novels *Skein of
Shadows* and *The Shard Axe*

A CUP OF JOE

978-148404-0874

Gini Koch

Want to know the untold story of Gini Koch? Did Gini really spend time in the Peace Corps? And did she really get arrested for stalking Nathan Fillion? Is she fluent in any language other than sarcasm? And what's the real reason she's banned from Denny's? The answer to these and other burning questions are in this book! So what are you waiting for? Buy this book NOW! It's not getting any younger, you know. Is it fact or fiction? You decide.

"I laughed. I laughed until I snorted soda pop out my nose, and my cats ran for cover."
– Word of the Nerd

RANDOM MUSINGS
FROM THE FUNNY GIRL
978-1-4952-4859-7

Gini Koch
writing as
Anita Ensal

BOONDOCKS FANTASY
(anthology from DAW Books)
"Being Neighborly"
978-0-7564-0653-0

LOVE AND ROCKETS
(anthology from DAW Books)
"Wanted"
978-0-7564-0650-9

Gini Koch

The Martian Alliance Chronicles

Join the crew of the Hummingbird as they take on the rich, famous, and sleazy of the galaxy. They're also on a long-term secret mission, so it's a good thing they're the best con artists, spacers, and roughnecks in the Milky Way, because they're going to need all their skills to ensure the Martian Alliance wins the war and saves the day.

THE ROYAL SCAM
Coming July 2015
ebook only

THREE CARD MONTE
Coming August 2015
ebook only

A BUG'S LIFE
Coming September 2015
ebook only

Gini Koch
writing as
G.J. Koch

The Alexander Outland Series
from Night Shade Books

In space, no one can hear you scheme…

"In the grand tradition of Harry Harrison's *Stainless Steel Rat*,
G.J. Koch introduces us to Captain Alexander Napoleon
Outland and his ribald and vibrant crew taking the universe
by storm… A humorous romp with twists and turns aplenty."
– Michael A. Stackpole,
author of *At the Queen's Command* and *Of Limited Loyalty*

"Laugh-out loud, read until you drop, Alexander (the)
Outland is my favorite space pirate."
– Patricia Briggs,
author of the Mercy Thompson series

Sometimes piracy just doesn't pay.

ALEXANDER OUTLAND: SPACE PIRATE
978-1-5978-0423-3
Also in audio!

Short Stories
from Gini Koch

CLOCKWORK UNIVERSE: STEAMPUNK VS. ALIENS
(anthology)
"A Clockwork Alien"
978-1-9407-0900-0

UNIDENTIFIED FUNNY OBJECTS 3
(anthology)
"Live at the Scene"
978-0-9884-3284-0

TWO HUNDRED AND TWENTY-ONE BAKER STREETS
(anthology)
"All the Single Ladies"
978-1-7810-8222-5

THE X-FILES: TRUST NO ONE
(anthology)
"Sewers"
978-1-6314-0278-4

Short Stories
from Gini Koch
writing as
J.C. Koch

THE MADNESS OF CTHUHLU VOLUME 1
(anthology)
"Little Lady"
978-1-7811-6452-5

A DARKE PHANTASTIQUE
(anthology)
"Outsiders"
978-0-9841-6765-4

KAIJU RISING: AGE OF MONSTERS
(anthology)
"With Bright Shining Faces"
978-0-9913-6056-7

Made in the USA
Coppell, TX
11 February 2020

15708589R00046